ART GALLERY AWAKENING

GAY PUBLIC SEX SERIES #8

NICO FOX

CONTENTS

CHAPTER 1

THEIR EYES WASH over my body. Their stare pierces my skin. Their lust scrutinizes every inch of me.

Standing naked in front of a room full of amateur artists never gets old. It never loses its rush either. I've removed my clothes in front of hundreds of people for classes like this. But the first couple of seconds are awkward, no matter how many times you do it.

The moment the robe comes off and the cool air hits my skin feels like my body is radiating energy. Hairs prickle at full mast. I settle into my most confident power stance. It's liberating.

Standing naked for a session is second-nature for me. But for those taking a drawing class for the first time, it's a bewilderment. Every time, they gasp and giggle at a man letting it all hang out five feet in front of them. I find it entertaining to witness their reaction.

This is my first-time modeling for an all gay male class. The instructor is hot as hell. He's young and tall with dark hair and a day's worth of stubble. He goes by Dorian Wilde, but I'm pretty sure that's not his real name.

It's a bit unnerving to be naked in front of such a tantalizing teacher. I'm used to being the most attractive person in the room, the object of desire. I'm sure many of the students wouldn't mind seeing the teacher up there.

Dorian talks to the class about shading and contrast. He points to my naked body and discusses how light reflects off of the muscles of my chest and arms. I keep breathing slowly, enjoying the praise.

This gig forces me to keep up with my workouts. But I'm no fool. I know the real reason why this studio keeps calling me back for sessions. There are plenty of muscular athletic guys willing to do this for a few extra bucks. But I have an eight-inch advantage.

The patterns in which their eyes move is comical. They look at my chest, then my penis. Then my arms, then my penis. Then my ass, then my penis. There is definitely one focus point on this subject.

I stand confidently and let my penis hang. That's 99 percent of what they want to see. This is an easy pose.

The hardest part of nude modeling isn't being naked. It's the poses. Standing still for a living sounds easy but holding your arms over your head for 10 minutes without moving is tiring.

Classes like this don't require difficult poses. It's the advanced classes that need me to bend and flex and hold those poses for a long time.

As the class draws me, I remember my journey to becoming a nude model. It started out as a dare, and I'm never one to back down from a dare. Then, when the instructor handed me $75 in cash, I realized this could be an easy side gig.

I've been posing naked for classes at this studio for two years now. It's helping to pay for college. But it's not just the money. Maybe I'm a bit of a narcissist and like to be the center of attention. Who am I kidding? I love the adoration.

"Connor, could you please move into the next pose," the Dorian tells me.

For this one, I clasp my hands behind my back and puff out my chest. I count 25 people in the class tonight. My tips will be awesome.

Tonight's class is for people who have never drawn anything before, let alone a naked person. I don't expect artistic excellence, but for many people who live busy lives, this may be the only artistic thing they do all year.

"The human form is unique to draw," he says. He goes on about spacing and relativity between lines. Funny, after all this time of listening to teachers explain the basics, I still don't understand what he's talking about. I'd never picked up a sketching pencil myself.

An older man in the second row squints to see me. Dorian notices and invites him to walk to the front for a closer observation of the muscles of my body. I'm not sure if he was faking poor eyesight just to get closer to me. Not that I mind.

"Look but don't touch," Dorian jokes, and the class laughs. I'm not supposed to move, but I can't help but smirk. He walks closer to me, using his thumbs and fingers to make a square picture frame around my crotch.

"Zone in on the erogenous zone," Dorian says, and I almost bust my load right in front of the class. The poor man is so embarrassed that he heads back to his easel. I like to think of myself as more than just a model. I'm helping people to get out of their comfort zones and grow as people.

This is much more light-hearted than last night's bachelorette party. Every single one of those women were drunk and touched my penis. I might have liked it more if I were into women, but it flattered me none-the-less.

Last night's art teacher was not as easygoing as Dorian is. He was a curmudgeon old man that wasn't even happy to be teaching the class. He kept warning them about model etiquette and threatened to kick them out. The bride-to-be threw in a $300 tip, so I had no complaints.

"Grab the pole, Connor." I grab a white plastic rod and hold it in my hand. One end sits on the floor, while the other is just a few inches taller than me. It helps the artist understand perspective. I place my feet on the two blue duct tape Xs on the stage and turn my head slightly to the side.

The artists put down their pencils and pick up their chalks and start drawing me in the new medium. More stares run up and down my body. This is usually the point in the evening where the amusement of seeing a naked person wares off and the students become more involved in their artwork.

We take a 10-minute break and I cover myself with the plush cotton robe. Students invite me to walk around and see their artwork. Some of them are pretty good for amateurs, much better than I could do. Not to mention that they're on their third round of champagne. More than a few of the students accidentally brush against me as I walk by.

A middle-aged guy laughs as I come closer to his canvas. His friends gather around him and cackle as they look at his piece. He had overdrawn the size of my penis so that it was bigger than my torso. It's hilarious.

The older guy who came up to me for a closer look earlier is next as I walk around the room. He is by far the best artist in the class. I don't think tonight is his first time drawing, like the others. The proportions are even, and my face looks very realistic. Just one problem. He drew underwear on me even though I was naked on stage. To each their own.

Dorian gathers the class back to their seats and pours some more champagne for everyone.

"I think this class is ready for something a little bit more provocative," he says in a suggestive tone. He looks at me and smirks. "Let me choreograph a new pose."

He nods for me to help him lift a comfy Lay-Z-Boy chair onto the stage. Usually my sitting poses are on a box or a folding chair, so this is a welcome change. Talk about a cushy job!

"Sit down and spread your legs wide."

My balls rest on the soft fabric. A small pearl glistens at the end of my penis. Dorian grins when he notices and grabs a paper towel. He seizes my member and cleans off the spot while the class looks shocked. He holds it for a beat before letting it fall back into place.

"Connor, for your first pose, cup your hand under your testicles and grab the base of your dick with the other."

I chuckle out loud at the notion. This is the first time during a modeling session someone had asked me to be overtly sexual. I feel a minor stirring down there.

By the time I grab myself, I'm already semi-hard. This is also the first time I'd had an erection while modeling before. The jaws of several students drop to the floor.

"The human body is always in motion," Dorian says. "A penis is constantly changing shape throughout the day. Capturing change is the essence of drawing the male nude."

The whole class is staring at my erection. I've never felt this exposed before.

"Erections are nothing to be scared of." he rests his hand on my shoulder and I feel a jolt of electricity through my loins.

He looks down at my length and nods approvingly while I touch myself. "That's exactly what we need. Once you are fully erect, rest your hands at your side," He stares intently into my eyes while his hand remains on my shoulder.

No other art teacher would get away with this in a studio. But this all-gay class isn't complaining. I just wish I knew what to expect when they hired me for this modeling session. It's exhilarating to be in front of these appreciative students with a full erection.

"Take notice of how the shape of Connor's torso changes when sitting in a chair as opposed to standing." His hands run down my chest and over my abs. I think he's trying to keep me hard for the class. It's working.

My cheeks feel a little warmer each time I catch him lingering over my body. I am fully throbbing now. From the look of Dorian's bulge, so is he. So many eyes focus on my protruding organ.

Chalk scratches against the canvas paper as students get to work. I blank out and feel detached from my erection, yet at the same time, enjoy the thrill.

"Time's up! Drop your chalk and look at your neighbors work."

Dorian hands me my robe, and I put it on despite still being hard. The students notice and are pleased to see the tent in the robe. It takes a few minutes before I soften underneath.

The class leaves, and several of the students drop bills in the tip jar. I get dressed behind the divider.

"You seem to have enjoyed that," he says.

"So intense."

"I think I have another experience that you might enjoy," he says. "You're the most popular model at this art school. You've gained quite the reputation."

"Just glad to have the cash continue to pour in."

"I'm debuting a new performance piece at a new art gallery dedicated to gay sex."

I furrow my brows at him. I'm shocked that such a thing exists. But intrigued.

"It's my big feature in two weeks, showing off my work in all sorts of mediums: graphic, oil, acrylic, and sculpture. I'll be selling my work and creating a work live in front of the crowd that will be auctioned off. All proceeds will go to the gallery. I'd like you to be the subject for my opening night exhibit."

"Does it pay as much as modeling for a class?"

"Ten times as much as long as you don't mind getting stiff in front of a crowd." He pauses. "And more."

That *and more* is too enticing to pass up. Tonight was so arousing that I want to take it even further.

I can tell he wants me and I'm pretty sure he knows that I want him too. And the students have left. I let my robe fall to the floor.

He gets on his knees like he's going to suck me off. Finally, Relief. He kisses my cock and gives it a little tug. "I can't wait to make you come in front of a live audience. But not now. Save all your sexual energy for the show."

He walks away leaving me with a serious case of blue balls.

CHAPTER 2

THE ART GALLERY is hidden away in a non-disclosed place. Nobody walking past it on the street would know it was there. The instructions say to take the back alley to get to the front door.

I walk in to see a sign that says, "Los Angeles Gay Sex Gallery." Underneath is a placard stating, "Leave your inhibitions at the door. This art gallery is dedicated to art that starts a sex positive conversation about societies attitudes towards the male nude and male sexuality."

The security guard spots me standing in line and guides me to the front. Everybody has to sign a waiver stating they are not offended by nudity or sexual situations and that they know what they are getting themselves into."

I walk around looking at various paintings of men ejaculating, photographs of men getting blow jobs, and sculptures of erect penises with hands wrapped around them. Everything has an underlying eroticism to it.

This crowd of gay men of all ages love it. None of them pay any attention to me as I hadn't yet been introduced as the "subject."

There are pieces from many different artists. The featured exhibit for Dorian Wilde is in the back area, where there is a stage, food buffet, and an open bar. Some of his paintings are sexual, others are both sexual and dark and make you feel conflicting emotions.

I take a shot of tequila for liquid courage. Dorian didn't tell me all the details of what I'd be doing. He said that if he told me, the element of surprise would be lost, and that model anticipation was key to the performance.

Lights flicker and then lower. The crowd gathers in front of the stage. Through a side curtain, out comes Dorian, completely nude, and he stands in the spotlight. The crowd cheers and claps and he waits for them to hush before speaking.

Dorian's cock is just as big as mine. He's got a nice swimmer's build, toned and trim. He won't have difficulty keeping me erect.

"Gentlemen and gentlemen. Welcome to the opening of California's first art gallery dedicated solely to gay sex." More hoots come from the audience.

He continues, "I stand naked in front of you to start an intimate exploration of art that represents our lives. As you know, they banned my last exhibit of erotic art after certain prudes complained to the city council. So much for our so-called cultured city." A few guys booed. "This exhibit will force you to confront your feelings about the male nude, desire, and longing to be seen for who we are."

The security guard meets me by the side and tells me to follow him. Dorian waves for me to come on stage. I thought he wanted me to pose nude in front of the audience.

"My lovely guests, this is Connor, my subject and model for the evening." They applaud for me. "Don't worry, pretty soon, he'll be naked too." I get some whoops from the audience. "In the meantime, feel free to have a snack, a drink or three, and of course, purchase some art." Everybody laughs. "The show will start in a half hour."

Thirty minutes of anticipation builds within me. I'm fully clothed and guests walk by me, presumably imagining me naked.

Dorian walks around the exhibit naked and talks to them about his work. It's one thing to stand naked as a silent subject in an art class, but to hold a normal conversation with confidence is even more erotic.

The lights flicker again, and I am ushered behind the stand where I am instructed to take off all my clothes. Here we go.

CHAPTER 3

I WALK on to the stage naked to feel the glare of the spot-light and hundreds of eyes on me. The excitement is over-whelming. Dorian, still naked, carries an easel and some paintbrushes onto the stage. The audience follows his member as it swings back and forth.

Cameras from the audience flash. I'd never had pictures taken of me during a modeling session. Something about being captured on film in all my glory awakens me. The thought that they can see me naked at any time is thrilling.

Dorian puts his hands on my shoulders and guides my body into the pose that he wants. He turns my head to look away from the video camera on the side of the stage. I didn't know he'd be filming this performance.

My mind jumps back and forth between Dorian's hot body and being naked in front of an audience. He's getting hard and I long to hold it in my hand.

"Chin up, chest forward," he says. "Don't look down."

He's not touching my girth. And I'm not touching myself. I can't see it, but I feel the energy channeling through my shaft.

To my right, the mob of testosterone is reacting to my growth. They're getting antsy and some are even licking their lips.

My face feels hot. Could I actually be embarrassed? Me, who's been posing nude for two years? I just had to stand there and let them watch my body respond.

I'm certain I am hard when I feel it twitch. He rubs my shaft with lube, and I look down, ready to spew for the crowd.

"Chin up, I said." He steps back to look me up and down as if I were one of his art pieces and he's examining it for worth. His brows crinkle as if he's concentrating on something. But what? He's seen me naked already.

He puts his hands on my hips and twists my pelvis a half inch to the side while I keep my upper body straight.

"That's it."

He walks back to his easel and looks me over again before picking up the paint brush. I can only see part of him out of the corner of my eye. Without thinking about it, he makes quick strokes with the brush. This is a pro at work.

He stands up and looks back and forth between the painting and me several times before giving a satisfied smirk. He turns the painting to the audience as they applaud.

"You can relax now," he says to me. "Let's give a hand for our handsome model." The crowd applauds. He bows, as if he were the star of a play. I give a short bow too, because I don't know what the protocol is for this kind of performance.

The painting is magnificent. The colors pop out from the canvas. It has several shades of peach and brown that highlight my skin tone. The arcs and bends of the picture match that of my body.

I want him to grab my flesh in front of the audience again. Maybe this is the part where he gets me off. I want to fuck him right on that stage, give the people their money's worth.

"And now for my signature." He picks up a tiny brush and throws it back on the table.

He lowers a bowl of paint down to his crotch and submerges his genitals in bright red paint. He presses his package against the lower right-hand corner of the painting, making sure to get a good impression of the cock head. I'm so hungry for his shaft that I can't stand it any longer.

"Acrylic paint takes about a half hour to dry. After that, Connor will put his signature on it. I'll seal it and we'll auction it to the highest bidder."

I can't wait to rub my dick in his paint. But I wonder why he can put his signature on it now, while I have to wait until it dries.

CHAPTER 4

WE TAKE a break while the guests grab some food and look at more artwork. Dorian doesn't bother to wash the paint off his junk before walking back into the crowd. He goes about his business of schmoozing patrons into buying more of his work.

We both walk through the gallery naked. Many of the guests get touchy-feely, but I don't mind. I love the attention and Dorian seems to like it too.

Dorian has his pieces to talk with the guests about. But I don't know what to say. When posing nude, the rule is that we're not allowed to talk. Models are just the subject of the art.

Guests ask me how often I work out and want to squeeze my bicep. One guy asks if I do private modeling. I tell him, "For the right price," and wink at him.

Dorian walks back towards me and caresses his hand against my thigh. I want to melt.

"I hope you're going to take care of me and not leave me hanging like you did at the art studio." I stare him in the eyes.

"And disappoint our guests?" He laughs before walking back to the stage.

His assistants follow him with a table, bowls, and other materials. He pours some powder and water into a bowl and mixes vigorously. As he shakes, his cock moves back and forth, and the audience loves it.

"Artists are always looking for new materials to work with," Dorian says. "I've developed a new type of silicone that dries within a couple of minutes. And no, I won't share my special blend with other artists." He laughs.

"While I mix this, I'll need a volunteer from the audience to keep our model Connor rock solid." Twenty or so hands go up. Dorian points to a cute blond twink in the front row who gets on stage.

The blond grabs my thickness and starts to stroke it and it feels so good to be touched in front of the audience. Dorian continues to stir his mixture.

He pulls out a tube slightly larger than my phallus and pours the liquid in.

"Thank you to our volunteer." He pulls me over to him and puts the tube over my length. The warm, lumpy liquid feels good surrounding my cock. It's similar to a blow job, but the sensation is much more intense.

Dorian twists the tube around my cock and moves it side-to-side before stopping. "Perfect. Now don't move for 5 minutes."

I can feel it hardening around my cock, which worries me. Will it stick to my skin?

A timer goes off and he drags the tube off my flesh as the *oohs* come from the crowd.

"See, good as new." Dorian grabs my prick and rubs his hands over it to show the audience that the material is completely gone.

Dorian sets the spongy mold to the side. He mixes hot pink powder into another bowl and fills the mold of my penis.

"The mold is dry, but it's going to take a couple more minutes for the silicone to form within the mold. In the meantime, who wants to see some more artwork of our beautiful Connor?"

The crowd cheers and I've never felt so admired.

Dorian has me sit in a folding chair next to his pot of clay. He puts his hands around my hard phallus and examines its size and shape, feeling every contour. I can't help but stay hard.

I want more than anything to come in his hands in front of this audience, but he won't let me. Instead, he focuses on molding the clay into the shape of my cock.

When he finishes, he puts the clay sculpture next to me for the audience to see. The replica is astonishingly similar.

"Who would like a clay version of Connor's penis? Bidding starts at $500."

The auction went on until it reached $1200. It's so electrifying to think that my cock will sit on some rich guys' shelf and he'll look at it every day.

The sexual tension is too intense. I yearn to orgasm. The gazes over my body, the cheers, the feel of Dorian's hands around my cock is all too much. I want to come, now.

"Let's check back at the table to see if our silicone is dry." He picks up the tube and pulls out a pink version of my dick and waves it in front of the crowd. Like the clay, he puts it up to my real dick and compares.

"You'll be amazed at how realistic this feels." Dorian walks up to the audience and lets them grab it and feel it. "Hold on. We need a comparison. Connor, come up to the audience so they can compare."

One by one, members of the audience grab my cock and then the pink silicone dildo. They're amazed at how realistic they are. I touch it myself and still can't believe it.

More amazing is how good it feels to have members of the audience fondle me. I love being their object of desire.

"You can purchase a replica of Connor's manhood in the gift shop. For those who place your orders tonight, we can ship yours out by the end of the week." He hands the mold and the pink dildo to his assistant. "And what you do with it after that is none of my business." We all laugh.

He shakes his hips so his massive cock waves to the audience. He grabs his dick at the base and circles it around in a helicopter. "Don't worry folks, you can buy a copy of my penis too." They hoot and holler.

I want Dorian to suck me off in front of the crowd. No, I want to hear their cheers as my girth enters his hole in front of each and every one of them.

CHAPTER 5

I CAN'T BELIEVE I've sustained a hard-on for this long. It's been over an hour. My balls are tight, and I want to come.

"One last time. I invite everybody to walk by and grab anything you want on our beautiful model before we finish the evening."

Dorian nudges me toward the end of the stage. Guys thrust their hands in the air for the chance to fondle my dick and ball sack. Some rub my legs, others my feet. Hands are everywhere on my body.

Why is he torturing me like this? Why won't he let me come?

Finally, he wraps his hand around my cock and strokes me up and down with a warming oil that tingles but feels so good. Each time I'm about to come, he stops and looks at me with a devilish grin. He's so evil.

"I put my signature on the painting when I pressed my genitals into the paint. Now we need Connor's signature."

There isn't any paint around.

He stands behind me, cock hard and rubbing up against my ass. I didn't know he wanted to fuck me, but I'll have it. He walks me up to stand next to the painting.

He penetrates me with his finger and rubs my prostate. I feel like I'm about to explode. He starts to jerk me off near the painting. The audience goes wild.

Just as I am about to explode, Dorian whispers to me, "Shoot it all over the painting."

I do as he says. My juice covers the painting from top to bottom. Little squirts miss the canvas and hit the floor, but for the most part, it's on the painting.

I wonder if I've ruined it. As I catch my breath, Dorian pushes me away from the painting and grabs a spray can and sprays a clear fixative over it.

He waves his hand over it twice and checks to see if it's dry before turning it back toward the audience.

"Voila! Connor's signature. Who wants this piece of Connor hanging in their home forever? Bidding starts at $3000." Someone in the audience shrieks.

I didn't think anybody would pay that much for a painting of me. Sure, it was a good painting, but three grand? To my surprise, it kept going up.

"Sold to our favorite philanthropist for $10,000. I'm sure our bidder will never forget our model's performance tonight."

Three waiters came out carrying trays of chocolate penises.

"We have a special surprise for all of you. While we were finishing the painting and auction, we used the mold of Connor's dick to make chocolate versions. Our chef has a famous freeze-drying method to make it snappy."

The patrons pick up the chocolate dicks off the tray but seemed weary about eating them.

"Don't worry, they're safe to eat. Enjoy putting your warm lips around Connor's dick."

This audience watched me stand naked in front of them and ejaculate. They've seen every inch of my body. Now they can imagine what it feels like to have my dick in their mouths. I think I'll get even more modeling gigs now.

ABOUT THE AUTHOR

Hi, I'm Nico. I love to write gay stories about public sex, cruising, bathhouses, anything taboo and a little bit dirty.

When I'm not writing, I love hanging out at the bars and binge-watching Netflix alike.

If you enjoyed this book, sign up for the Mailing List and receive a FREE book.

See you next time

-Nico

Join the Mailing List

For more information:
www.NicoFoxAuthor.com

ALSO BY NICO FOX

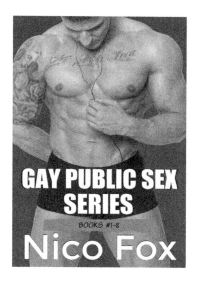

The complete Gay Public Sex Series box set. **Eight** steamy M/M erotic stories full of **public** encounters.

This bundle includes:

Bulge on a Train

Truck Stop Fantasy

Fitting Room Temptation

Ferris Wheel Threesome

Hole in the Wall Exhibitionist

Ride-Share Stripper

Gay Resort Weekend

Art Gallery Awakening

The first Jock Series box set. **Six** steamy M/M erotic stories full of **sweaty athletic guys**.

This bundle includes:

Captain of the Swim Team

First Time, First Down

Soccer Jockstrap

Slammed By the Team

Team Catcher

Heavyweight Punch

The first DILF Series box set. Six stories about **hot daddies** and their younger counterparts.

This bundle includes:

DILF of My Dreams

Seduced by the DILF

My Boss is a DILF

First Time Gay with My Girlfriend's Dad

My Girlfriend's Dad Wants It

First Time Gay with the DILF Professor

CRUSH ON MY STRAIGHT BEST FRIEND

Nico Fox

"I always follow his lead about anything and everything. All of our friends do. He uses his charm and imposing stature to convince us to do anything he wants."

Finn always had a crush on his best friend, Cameron, who is *very* popular with the girls. Standing next to well-built, captain of the football team, and all-around stud Cameron makes Finn feel a little, shall we say, less than…insecure.

Cameron has always protected Finn from others when they make fun of him for his small stature and he's always felt secure with him.

Finn invites Cameron over for a night of video games and beer only to be shocked when Cameron makes a wager on a game that Finn can't say no to. Who says fantasies don't come true?

My
BOSS
for
Christmas

Nico
Fox

Dustin has landed his dream job in Silicon Valley just one month after graduating college. He tries to keep his head down as much as he can, despite being surrounded by **hyper-masculine alphas** that call each other **bro.** He just can't stop lusting after the company's founder, notorious womanizer and billionaire's son, Brett.

The company is in peril. A bug in their software may cause one of their biggest customers to leave them. Everyone in the office is nervous, but they try to cover it up with heavy drinking after work and carrying on with their secret Santa ritual.

But Dustin solves the bug, making him the company hero. Brett is eternally grateful to his new employee for saving his company. Find out how this straight stud will pay back his employee in this new erotic story from Nico Fox.

A SEXY underground Halloween party…

"It's amazing how far two people in love will go to hide their inner desires from each other."

Lucas is a shy college student. His boyfriend, Colton, is an extroverted sports stud that every guy on campus wants to get with. Together, they have the perfect relationship. Or so it seems.

Lucas is worried someone will steal Colton away because he's such a catch. What's more, Lucas doesn't know if he can trust himself to handle monogamy.

They head into Manhattan to look for the perfect Halloween costumes for their upcoming school party. They want sexy costumes to show off all that hard work in the gym.

At the costume store, they meet Ace, a sophisticated New Yorker throwing his own Halloween party, one where inhibitions are thrown to the wind.

Ace seems a little shady. The party is so elusive that they need to be blindfolded as they ride in a limo to the party. But that's the price Lucas is willing to pay to go to a real New York City party.

How will Lucas and Colton's relationship hold up after a wild night at the party? Will jealousy get in the way, or will exploration bring their relationship to new heights?